Tonya & The Witch

Written by

Liberty Dendron

First Edit by Janice Johnson

First printing

ISBN:978-0-9817448-6-5

Published by: Mamba Books & Publishing

Dendron Virginia

Printed in the United States of America

Once upon a time, there lived a witch who was very mean. She was very ugly. She had only one daughter, who was named Tonya, and she was no nicer than her mother. The witch wanted to train her daughter in witch-craft, to follow in her footsteps. But, no matter how much the mother tried, Tonya was not he least bit interested. She never wanted to be bothered with witchcraft or castle work, either. She was only interested in looking beautiful.

Tonya was very worried about her looks and she spent most of her time in front of the lake, putting on make-up. She painted her face in colors and polished her nails. She did her hair up, every morning, evening and night, in every style she could think of. She wanted to look as pretty as possible; she never realized that what she did; sometime made her look bad.

One day, Tonya's mother had to visit a village down south. She ordered Tonya to cook the magic potion, which was on the fire, until she returned.

"Why should I have to do it?" Tonya complained.

"You know how much I hate making potions.

The big spoon spoils my nail polish, and the steam makes my make-up run."

"It has to be done!" said her mother, heading out the door.

"I will be back as soon as I can. In the meantime, keep stirring that pot!"

"It's not fair!" Tonya muttered. She picked up the big spoon and started to stir.

After a while, she heard an unfamiliar sound.

It sounded like a swarm of bees flying, overhead.

She looked up to see what it was. "Oh!" she cried. It's butterflies. Tonya's eyes glowed. "What beautiful creatures!

If I could be as beautiful as that!" she thought to herself, looking up at the butterflies.

"How did they become so beautiful? What is their secret," she thought. "If I could catch one, it could tell me its secret. Yes, I must catch one." She left the potion boiling on the fire, and ran into the castle to get the magic broom. But her mother had already gone away on it.

"Oh, no!" she muttered. She was very disappointed that she would not be able to catch the butterfly. She stood in front of the grape vine, sulking.

"Oh, how can I ever become as pretty as that?"
She thought and thought and thought, but
nothing came to her mind.

Suddenly, she got an idea. "Perhaps my
mother has a portion in her magic book, to make
me pretty, like a butterfly. Surely, she must
have one."

She ran into the hut, and straight to the
bedroom.

She looked everywhere in the bedroom, looking for
a formula, searching for a magic formula. But
she couldn't find a formula to become pretty,
like a butterfly. She was very disappointed.
She couldn't stop thinking about the pretty
butterfly.

She paced up and down angrily, not wanting to
give up.
"Well," she thought, "I will make a portion of
my own."

She went back to the tree, still trying to think up a formula. She became nervous and angry, because she couldn't think of anything. "What ingredients should I use to make that magic portion?" she asked herself. She thought and thought, but she just couldn't think of anything that would make her beautiful.

After a while, Tonya felt something pecking her leg. It was an Ostrich. "Stop," she said. The Ostrich pecked at Tonya. It seemed to be lonely. Tonya, who was already angry, became even angrier at that. "Stop!" she yelled.

When the Ostrich didn't leave, Tonya grabbed it by its neck and threw it on the ground. The poor Ostrich stood and ran away with her feathers flying everywhere.

At that moment, long ostrich feathers grew out from Tonya's body. She was so absorbed in thoughts of becoming as beautiful as a butterfly, she didn't feel them. She stirred the potion faster, thinking of the ingredients she should put in.

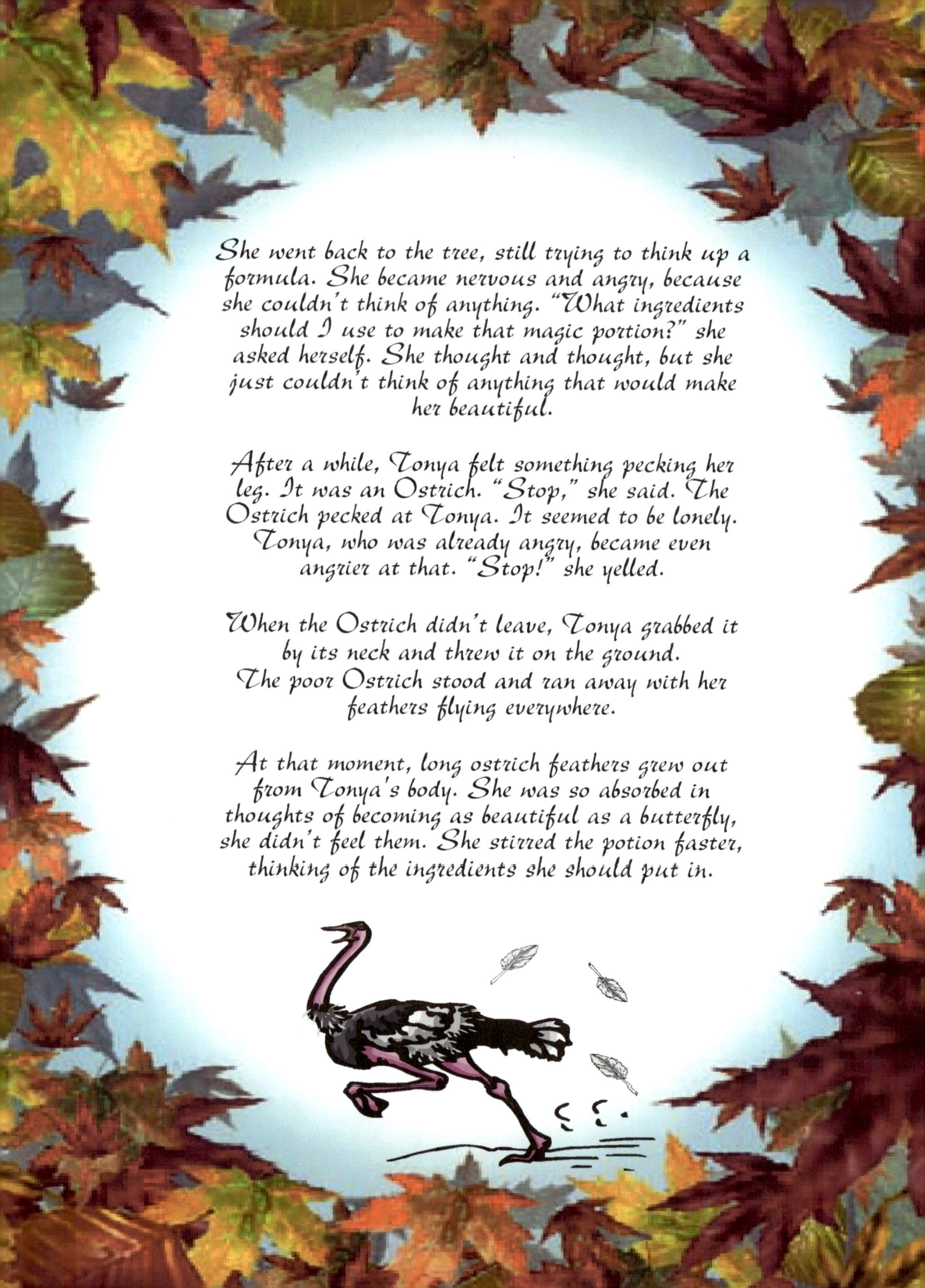

Then her dragon saw something strange hanging from Tonya's back and flew over to her, fire and smoke blazing. Thinking it was a threat, he pulled on it.

Tonya was angry about being disturbed again. She hit the dragon with the broom. The dragon's wing was hurt by the broom and some of the potion spilled on the ground, as well.

The poor dragon shrieked in pain and quickly limped away. Tonya was so mean, she didn't care that she had hurt the dragon. Nor did she feel sorry for him. She continued to stir the potion. Soon, sores popped out all over her body. But, she was so absorbed in thoughts of becoming beautiful, that she didn't notice them.

The Gnu, she were going to slaughter for dinner, smelled the potion that had been spilt on the ground. He got up from his bed of hay and came to lick it up, because he was so thirsty. This angered Tonya even more; she hit the Gnu with a stick. The poor, thirsty Gnu staggered away, in fear and pain.

And, in no time, she grew green spots just like that of the Gnu,
sprouted from her body and her hair became coarse and stiff, like hay.
But Tonya didn't notice it, because she was too busy, thinking about the ingredients she should put in her beauty potion.

The Buffalo in the lake saw Tonya's new beard and bristly hair. She was very hungry and thought that it was a stack of hay, so came to eat it.

Tonya, without realizing why the Buffalo came to her, angrily threw a stick of firewood at her.

It hit her on the horns and the poor hungry Buffalo ran away, mooing in fear. Within no time at all, two bumps emerged from the sides of Tonya's head and grew into two big horns. But, still she didn't notice!

When the Ostrich saw this strange creature, he didn't know it was Tonya. He sprang at her, snapping and pecking.
Tonya was very annoyed at him forsnapping at her, she hit the Ostrich with the brook. It hit the Ostrich on the mouth and the poor, stricken Ostrich ran away, howling.

Suddenly, Tonya's teeth fell on the ground, as she stirred the potion. But she didn't notice them because, she was too deep in thoughts of learning; how to become beautiful, like butterflies.

Monkey woke up, hearing the clamor. When he saw Tonya,

He was so frightened; he leaped up into the tree.

"Oh! Tonya," the monkey cried, "what happened to you? You've become uglier than ever. You're the ugliest person I've ever seen," the little monkey screeched, in terror. Tonya was furious.
She shook his tree and shouted ugly words at him. As she shouted,
her voice cracked and became hoarse, more like a croak, than a voice.

"Oh! What's wrong?" Tonya was very confused and felt that something was not right. She ran to the lake.

When she saw herself in the lake she was horrified. "Oh, no! No, " she screamed.

"Oh no, I wanted to be pretty like a butterfly." She ran out of the hut, screaming wildly. She was angrier than ever. She shouted and crawled on the ground, cursing the butterfly.

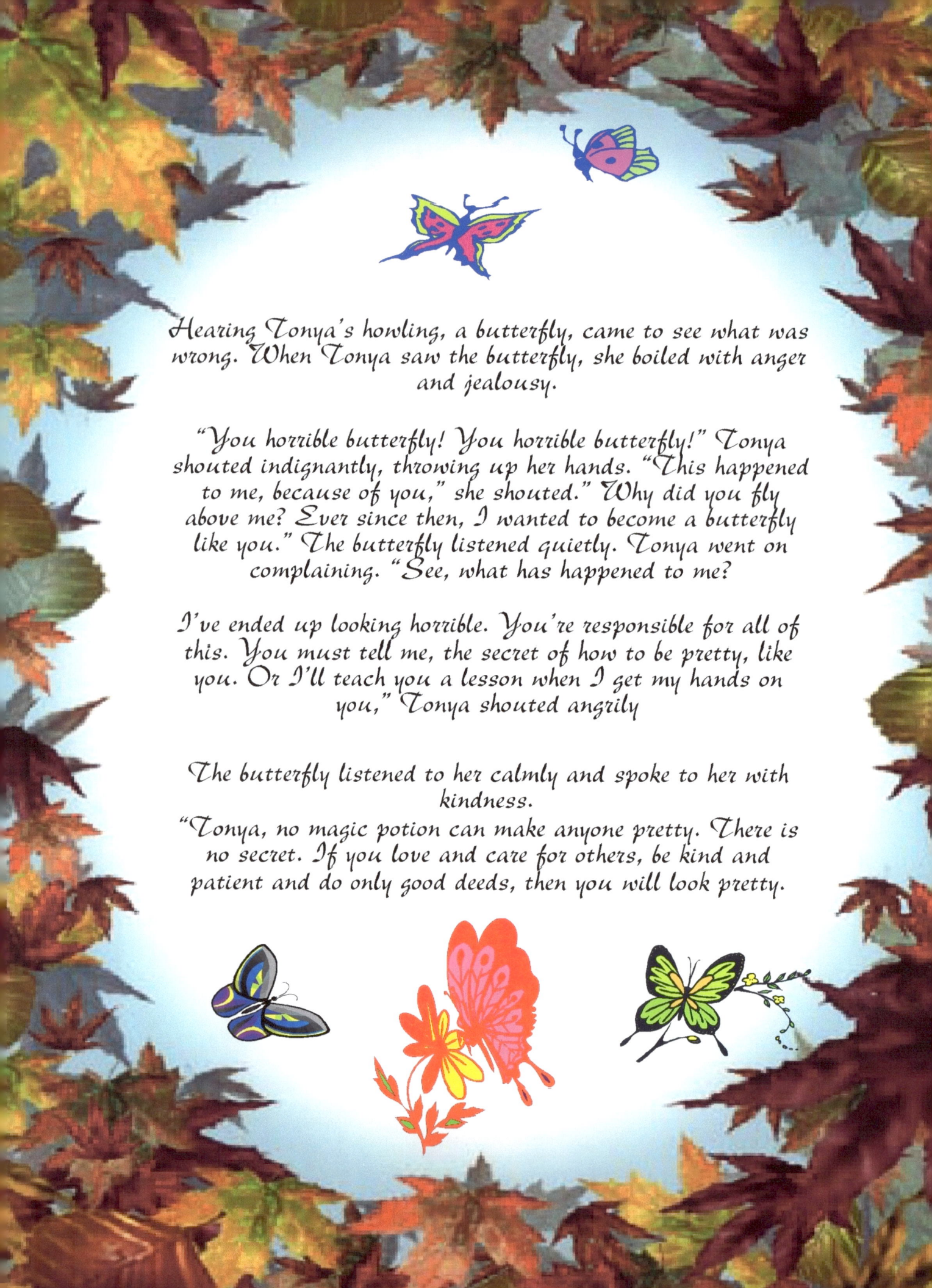

Hearing Tonya's howling, a butterfly, came to see what was wrong. When Tonya saw the butterfly, she boiled with anger and jealousy.

"You horrible butterfly! You horrible butterfly!" Tonya shouted indignantly, throwing up her hands. "This happened to me, because of you," she shouted." Why did you fly above me? Ever since then, I wanted to become a butterfly like you." The butterfly listened quietly. Tonya went on complaining. "See, what has happened to me?

I've ended up looking horrible. You're responsible for all of this. You must tell me, the secret of how to be pretty, like you. Or I'll teach you a lesson when I get my hands on you," Tonya shouted angrily

The butterfly listened to her calmly and spoke to her with kindness.
"Tonya, no magic potion can make anyone pretty. There is no secret. If you love and care for others, be kind and patient and do only good deeds, then you will look pretty.

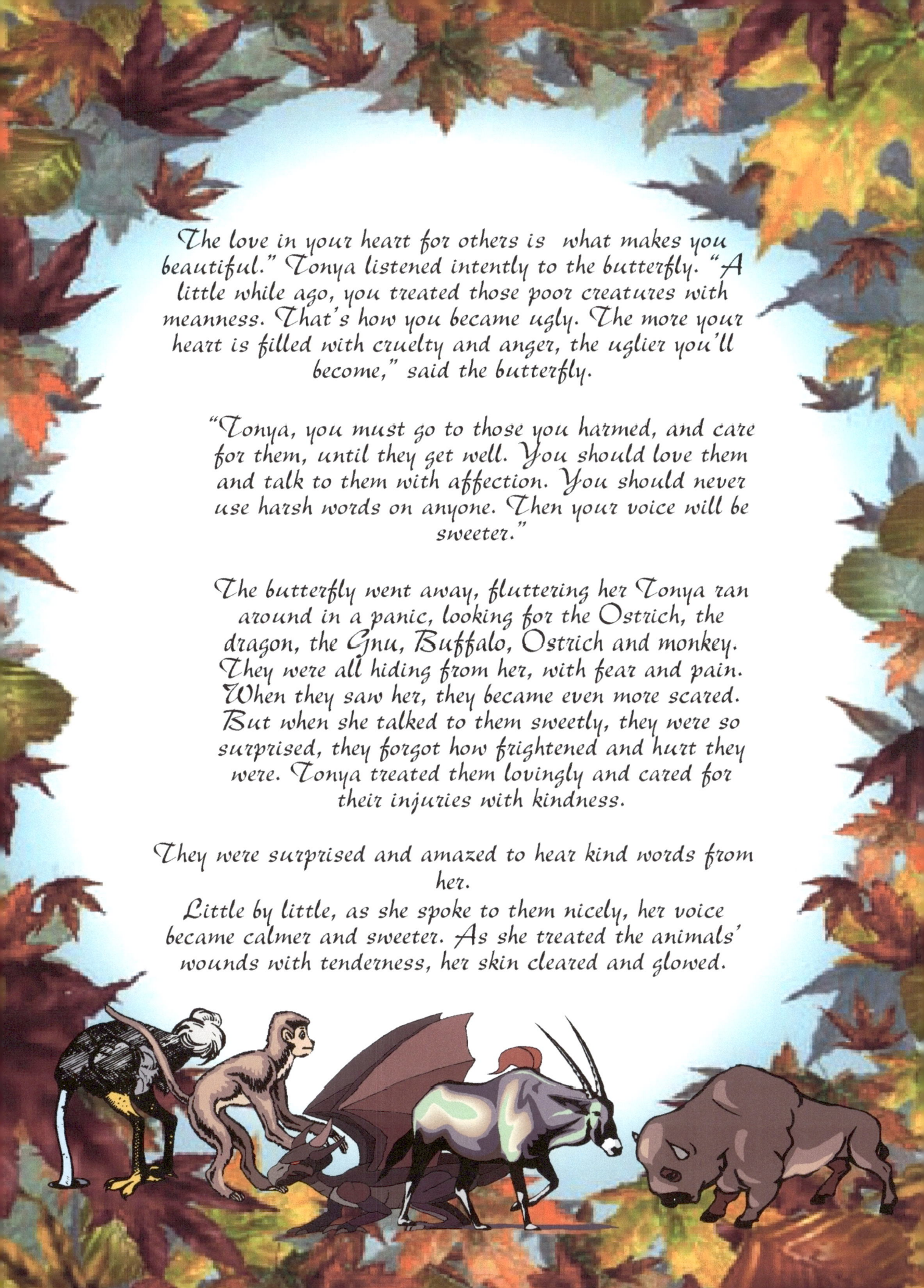

The love in your heart for others is what makes you beautiful." Tonya listened intently to the butterfly. "A little while ago, you treated those poor creatures with meanness. That's how you became ugly. The more your heart is filled with cruelty and anger, the uglier you'll become," said the butterfly.

"Tonya, you must go to those you harmed, and care for them, until they get well. You should love them and talk to them with affection. You should never use harsh words on anyone. Then your voice will be sweeter."

The butterfly went away, fluttering her Tonya ran around in a panic, looking for the Ostrich, the dragon, the Gnu, Buffalo, Ostrich and monkey. They were all hiding from her, with fear and pain. When they saw her, they became even more scared. But when she talked to them sweetly, they were so surprised, they forgot how frightened and hurt they were. Tonya treated them lovingly and cared for their injuries with kindness.

They were surprised and amazed to hear kind words from her.
Little by little, as she spoke to them nicely, her voice became calmer and sweeter. As she treated the animals' wounds with tenderness, her skin cleared and glowed.

When she nursed them with affection, her hair became soft and lustrous. When she looked at them with love in her eyes, her eyes became brighter and clearer. Little by little, she became pretty, just like the butterfly

Eventually, two little bumps appeared on her back and turned into lovely wings.

"Oh!" She cried, as happy as she could be. She flew up into the air, fluttering her wings. Tonya finally became a butterfly and flew above the trees. After that she was never unkind to anyone and was loved by all.

The End

"what are these colors"

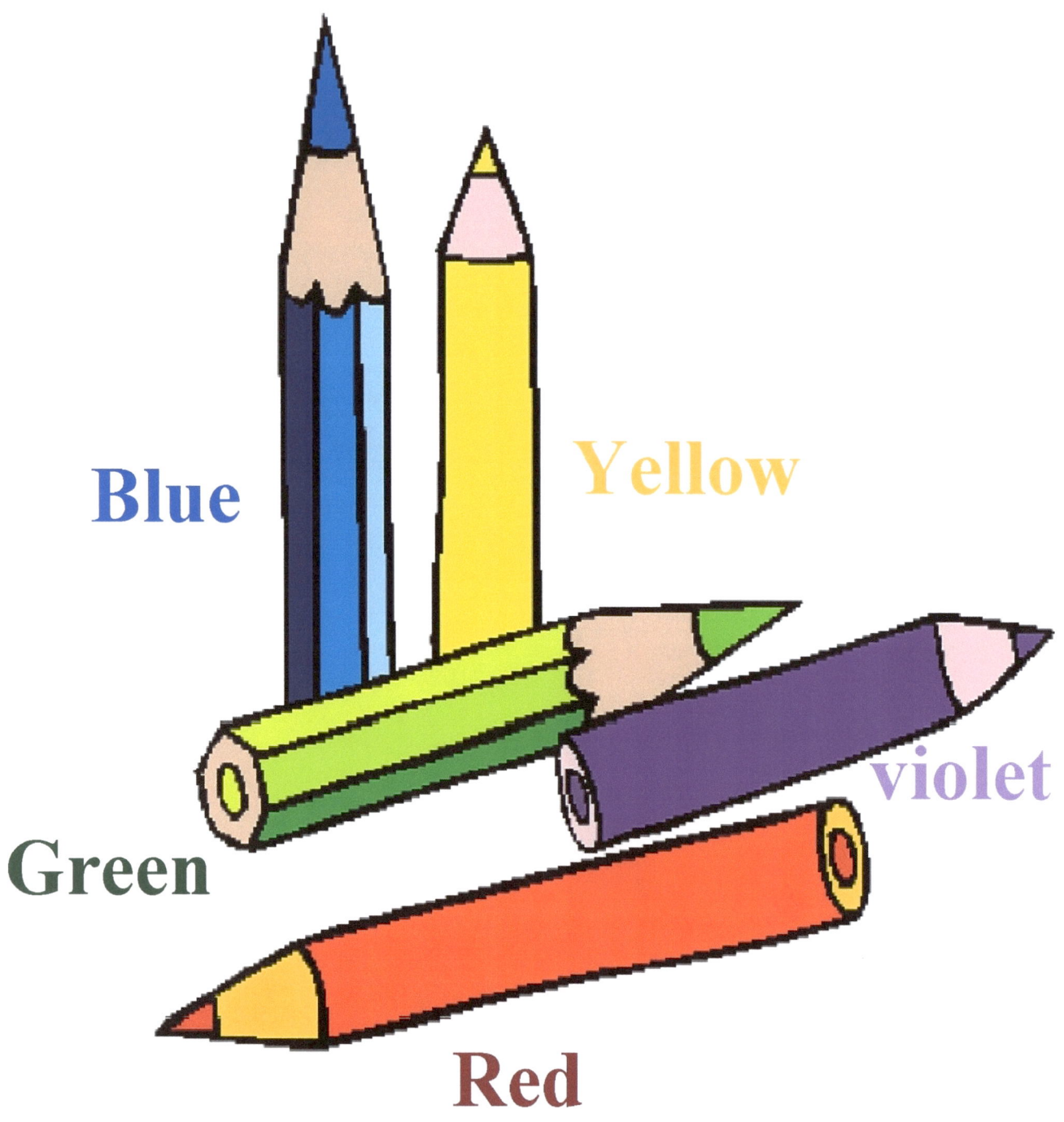

Blue

Yellow

Green

violet

Red

Bull__1
One
Wilderbeast

Gnu ___2
Two

Crane ___ 3
Three

Oryx___ 4
Four

Zebra__5
Five

Hippo__6
six

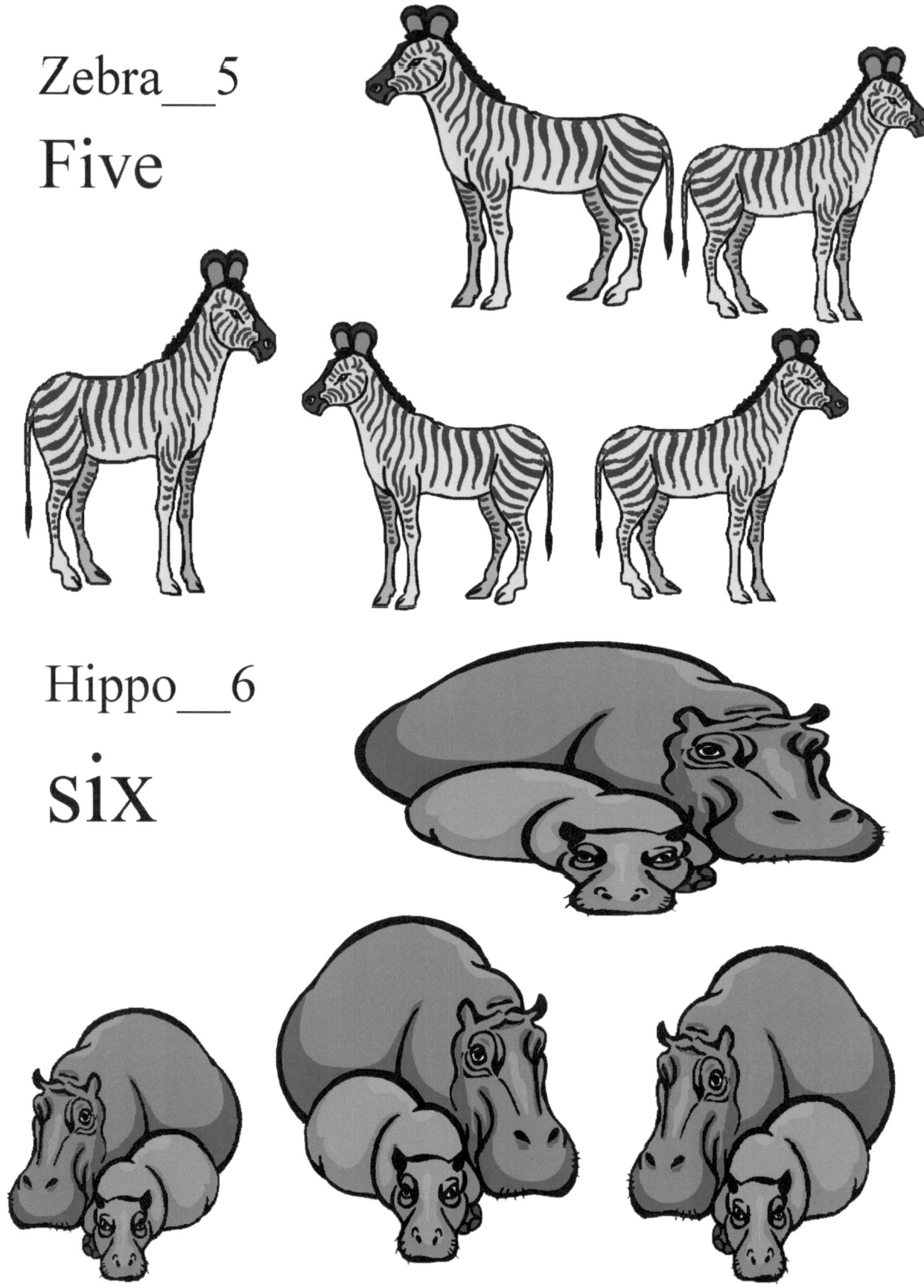

Hyena__ 7

Seven

Elephant__ 8

Eight

Hyena__ 7

Seven

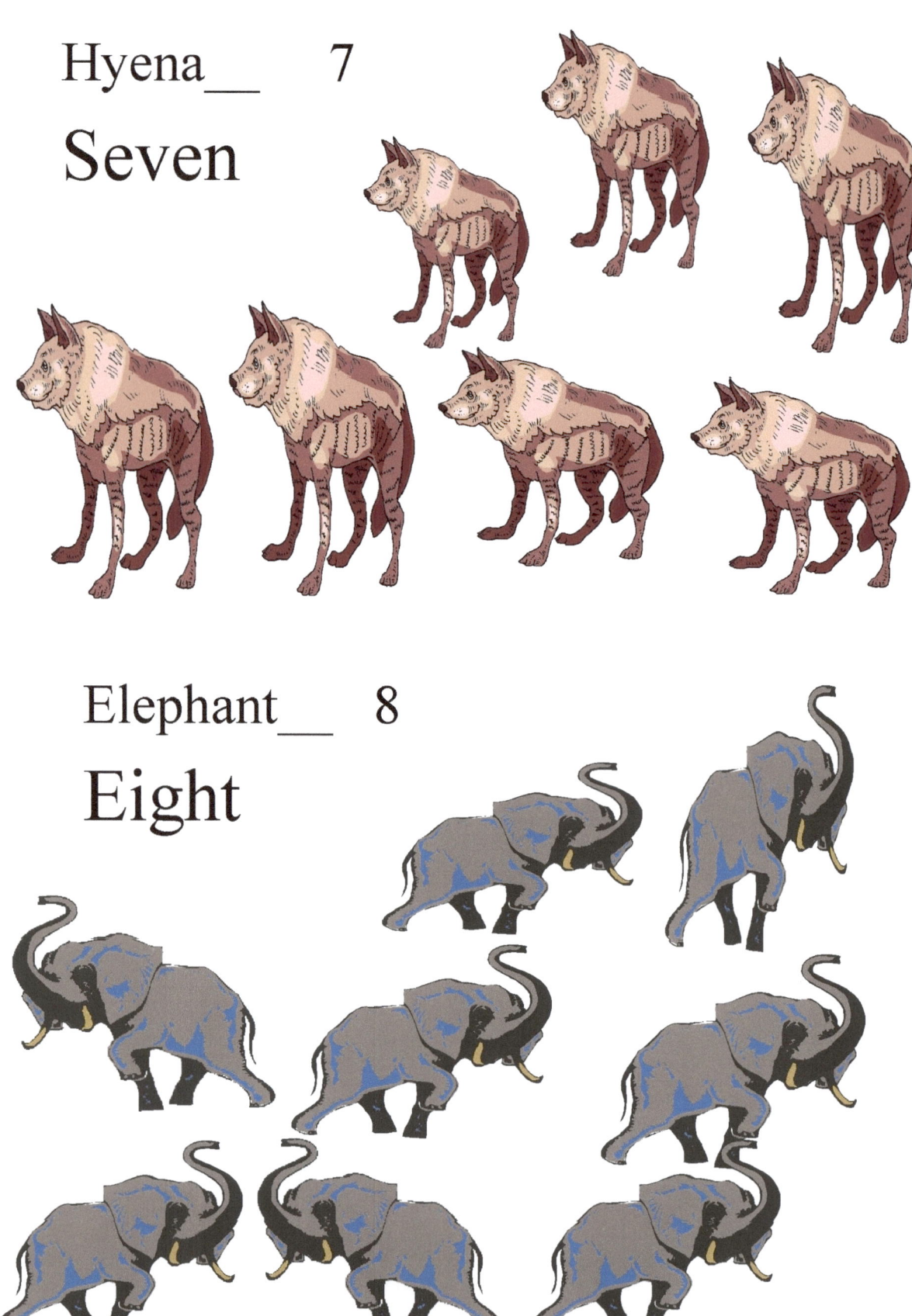

Elephant__ 8

Eight

BOOKS Written By!

Liberty Dendron

Monley & Hyena

by Liberty Dendron

Mamba Media Animal Alphabets

by Liberty Dendron

Great Escape

Written by Liberty Dendron

Giant Lizards And Friends

by Liberty Dendron

Fluffy Rabbit

by Liberty Dendron

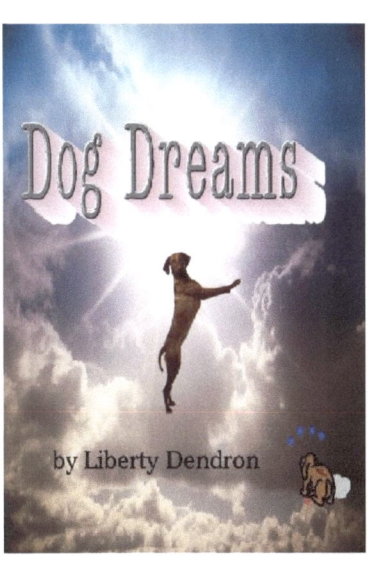

Dog Dreams

by Liberty Dendron

mambabooks.com

BOOKS Written By!

Books available by the author:

Liberty Dendron

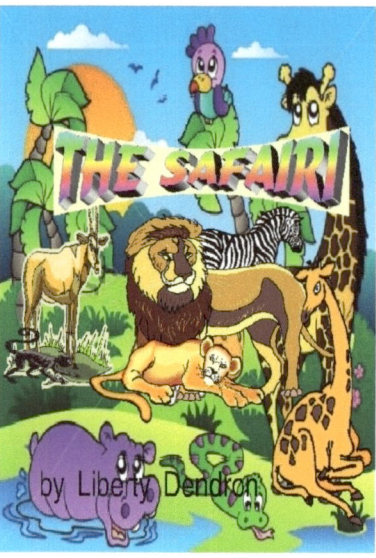

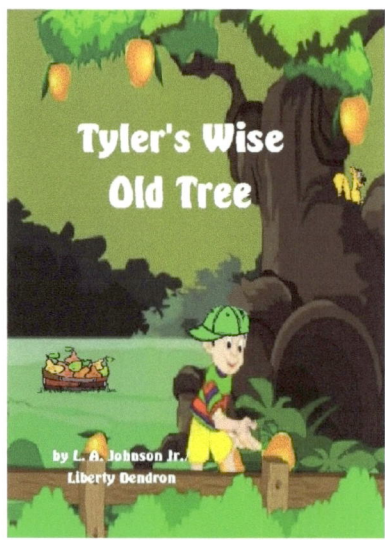
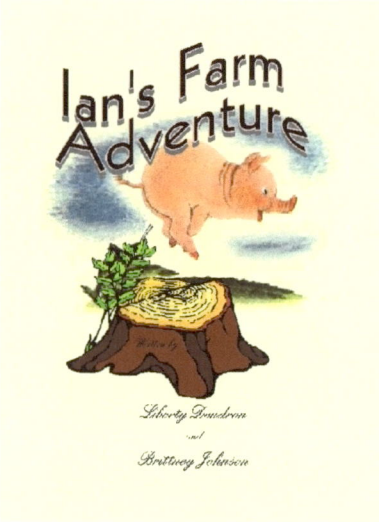

mambabooks.com

BOOKS Written By!

Liberty Dendron /or L A. Johnson Jr.

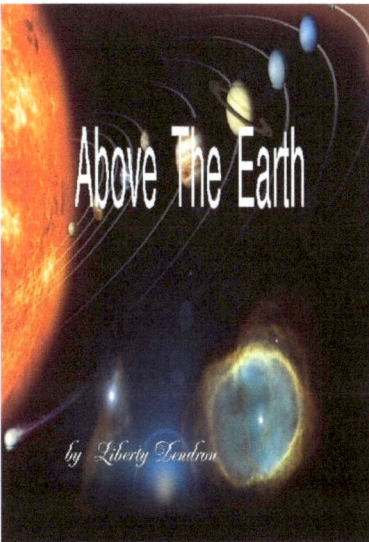

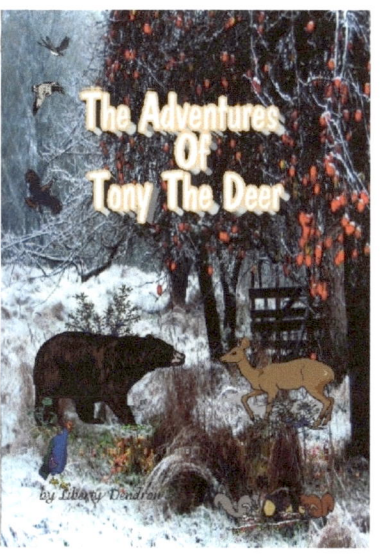

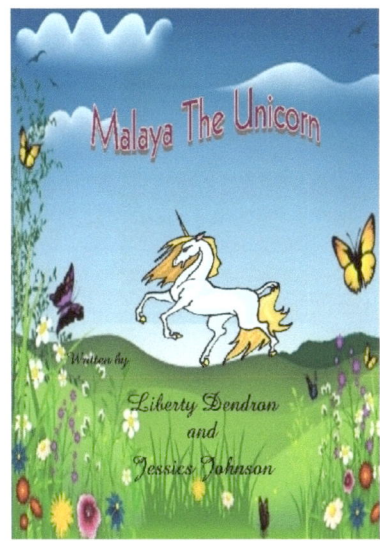

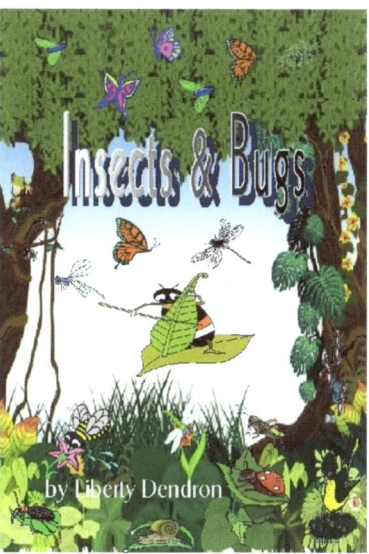

mambabooks.com

Lafayette A. Johnson Jr., Ph.D.
in Creative Writing,
Literature and English